The Legend of the
Lone Ranger™
Storybook

The Legend of the Lone Ranger™
Storybook

Random House New York

Lord Grade and Jack Wrather
Present
A Martin Starger Production

The Legend of the Lone Ranger
Starring
Klinton Spilsbury, Michael Horse,
Christopher Lloyd
Matt Clark, and introducing **Juanin Clay**
and
Jason Robards as President Ulysses S. Grant
Executive Producer **Martin Starger**
Original music by **John Barry**
Director of Photography **Laszlo Kovacs, A.S.C.**
Screenplay by
Ivan Goff & Ben Roberts and **Michael Kane**
and **William Roberts**
Adaptation by **Jerry Derloshon**
Produced by **Walter Coblenz**
Directed by **William Fraker**

Storybook adaptation by **Larry Weinberg**

An AFD/Universal Release
© 1981 Lone Ranger Television, Inc.
© 1981 ITC/Wrather Productions

Many years ago, a man on a great white horse galloped out of nowhere across the plains of Texas. Although he always wore a mask, he was not an outlaw. With his Indian friend, Tonto, he brought to justice the worst desperadoes who ever roamed the West.

Nobody knew who he was or where he came from. Nobody until now! For here at last is the story of the masked man of legend—the Lone Ranger.

Texas, 1854

One day, a crowd of Indian children came running into their village shouting, "Tonto's caught a prisoner! Tonto's caught a prisoner!"

"What? Our little Tonto?" cackled an old squaw. "What did he capture, a rabbit?"

"No! Look!" cried one of the boys, pointing past the line of tepees.

An Indian boy with a bow and a quiver of arrows on his back rode slowly in on his pony. Mounted on the pony behind him was another boy. He was not an Indian.

Chief Talking Bear, hearing the fuss, came out of his tent.

"This is no prisoner," Tonto said. "I saw white men raid his ranch. They shot his father with their long guns. And his mother, too, when she tried to save her brave. Then they burned his home and ran the horses off."

Frowns appeared on the grown-ups' faces. They wondered why an Indian boy should help a white boy. "We know what it is to have our homes destroyed by the white men," said Tonto. "I could not leave him there."

Tonto's father came forward through the crowd, calling to his son, "You have been told before to stay away from where the white men live. It is dangerous for an Indian. You have broken my rule."

A hand rested gently on the angry father's shoulder. "You are right, my friend," said Talking Bear, "to scold him for not using his head. But now that you have done so, is it not also right to praise him for using his heart?"

"Yes, you speak wisely," said the brave, for he was really proud of his son. "He hears the voice of the Great Mysterious. His new friend shall be welcome among us —and in our tepee."

Then the chief asked, "What is his name?"

The white boy could not answer for himself. He opened his mouth to speak but closed it again. He did not want to burst into tears.

"It is John," said Tonto, "John Reid."

Talking Bear studied the white boy's face, then turned to the others. "John Reid," said the chief, "needs time to know his sadness. Let us leave him to that which is crying inside of him."

Left to himself, John wandered slowly through the village. Everything was like a dream. He could not believe that his parents were gone forever. That his home was gone. When the other children looked at him, he did not see them, for his eyes were clouded.

The day grew late. The sun turned orange, then red, and seemed to grow bigger. It looked heavy, like John's heart, and it sank lower and lower in the sky.

All at once, Chief Talking Bear was standing beside him. "It is

true that you cannot see your parents, my son, but they are spirits now and they will always dwell inside of you. You cannot lose them unless you forget them, and a loving heart will not do that."

The clouds passed from John's eyes. He saw that the old chief was smiling. "Come now," said Talking Bear. "Learn our ways. Do not stand apart. Be one of us. There is much that awaits you."

Slowly at first, John entered the life of the village. Tonto's father taught him how to spear fish in the stream and to use a bow and arrow. Tonto's mother showed John how to find roots and berries in the desert weeds and brush. From Tonto's father, John learned to tell directions by the sun and the stars. Tonto and his friends taught John their games. Little by little, the boy who had lost his parents found himself becoming less unhappy.

One evening, all the villagers gathered. Something special was about to happen. John asked Tonto what was going on.

"Rain dance," said Tonto. "But only the elders can wear the masks."

"What masks?"

"The masks that bring the rain."

"Dancing and masks can't make it rain," said John in disbelief.

"Wait and see," said Tonto.

Soon the ceremony began. The tom-toms started to throb. Men, women, and children rose from where they sat on the ground and started to dance in a circle. As they did, they chanted a prayer to the rain spirits. John stood apart from them, watching. He could not take his eyes off the wild, fierce masks that the elders put over their faces.

Suddenly the sky darkened. There was a flash of lightning. Then rain came pouring down.

That night, John dreamed he had put on a mask of his own that helped him do wonderful things. He was chasing the bandits who had killed his parents. Soon he would catch them and . . .

He awoke. Tonto was leaning over him. "Time for the races," he said to John.

Tonto and John took their spears and joined the other young braves. They all mounted horses and divided into two lines. One brave at a time from each team raced up to a spear sticking out of the ground. He yanked it out and stuck his own spear in its place. Then he galloped off to rejoin his team at the other end of the line. Whichever team finished first would win.

Soon it was John's turn. Galloping at full speed, John hung over the side of his pony. He was ready to switch the spears. Suddenly he lost his balance and went flying off the horse, landing right on his behind.

All the other boys laughed — even Tonto. John got up quickly. He wasn't hurt, but he was so mad that he wanted to punch Tonto.

Then he heard the old chief's voice behind him. "Is it wise to fight a friend while you are angry? How, then, will you keep him your friend?" A moment later, John was laughing with the rest.

That night, around the campfire, Chief Talking Bear spoke to the young braves about the Great Mysterious. "I see," said the chief, "that the Great Mysterious cherishes everything that lives. I live, and so the Great Mysterious cherishes me. I listen to the voice that is in me. Then I, too, cherish all living things. If this is so, then have I not learned to be just?"

John did not understand everything that the great chief said, but he knew that someday he would.

As the weeks passed, John came to feel as if this Indian village was truly his home. Then one day, while he was wrestling with Tonto, a white man led his horse slowly in among the tepees. He wore the uniform of a lawman—a Texas Ranger. For a moment John simply stared. Then, in a flash, he recognized his brother, Dan.

Jumping off his horse, Dan Reid ran up to his younger brother and hugged him. Dan had been away in Mexico on Ranger business when the outlaws had attacked their parents' ranch. After his return, he had searched everywhere for John before he had thought of the Indians. He did not think they would befriend a white boy.

John was wildly happy to see his brother, until he realized that now he would have to leave the village. His brother had decided to send him back East to live with an aunt until he grew up.

John walked sadly through the village saying his good-byes. Finally, it was time to leave. Talking Bear looked into John's eyes and said, "You shall become a wise hunter . . . a brave warrior . . . a great man. You will seek what is just for all creatures that live."

When John turned at last to Tonto, the Indian boy took a silver amulet from his own neck and placed it around John's.

"From this moment and forever," said Tonto, "wherever you go, whatever you do, you will always be Kemo Sabe."

"What does that mean, Tonto?" asked John.

"Trusted friend," he answered.

Then John took out his hunting knife and made a cut on the palm of his left hand. Tonto did the same. The two boys clasped hands in farewell. They were blood brothers now.

Many times would the earth circle the sun before they saw each other again. . . .

Texas, 1870

Tonto grew to manhood without learning what had become of his Kemo Sabe. Perhaps they would never see each other again. John Reid might never return from the distant shores and cities of the East.

Then one day, a stagecoach came bouncing west along a bumpy prairie trail. The driver was taking his time because one of his lead horses was having a problem. "Marmalade's tooth is hurting her again," he told Shotgun, the man sitting next to him with the rifle. "She's trying to pull me to Mexico."

Before Shotgun could smile, gunshots rang out. He and the driver turned and saw four horsemen in gray hoods riding up fast behind them.

"Road agents!" shouted Shotgun.

"Here's what they pay us for,

kid!" said the driver. He cracked the reins. The horses went flying.

No matter how fast they went, the men on horseback kept gaining on them. Shotgun aimed and fired. He missed. He aimed again and hit a rider in the shoulder. But the outlaw didn't fall. Shotgun never got to pull his trigger again. An outlaw's bullet sent him spinning over the side of the stagecoach.

Now the driver was alone, trying to control the horses with one hand and shoot back with the other. A rider, galloping hard, came up on the driver's left side, his pistol blazing. The stagecoach driver fired carefully, and horse and rider went down together.

Soon the three other outlaws were alongside the stagecoach, firing from both sides at once. The driver slumped down, wounded. The reins fell from his hands, and the horses were on their own.

Wild with fear, they bolted. One of the outlaws, riding in close, leaped from his horse onto the runaway team. But before he could control them, the wounded driver fired. The outlaw slid to the ground as the stagecoach plunged ahead.

Now it looked as if there was nothing that could stop the stagecoach from crashing. The two remaining outlaws knew that all they had to do was tag along and wait for the coach to crash.

Suddenly, a young man in eastern clothes swung out the stagecoach door. It was John Reid! Quickly he climbed up over the top. Crouching low, he made his way over the wildly swaying carriage to the driver's seat and grabbed the reins. Then, knowing that he couldn't escape the outlaws, he pulled in on the reins and brought the runaway team to a standstill.

At gunpoint, the two outlaws ordered everyone to get off the stage. John helped the wounded driver down and turned over the saddlebag that the men demanded. They got what they had come for, but they were greedy. Maybe there was money in the passengers' bags. One of the outlaws began searching inside the coach.

This gave John his chance. In a flash, he leaped on the other outlaw. They both hit the ground together, but the outlaw managed to get to his feet. He began swinging his rifle like a club. John ducked and lashed out with his fists. The stunned man reeled backward, dropping the rifle. Hearing the scuffle, the other outlaw rushed out of the coach and leveled his gun straight at John. In another instant he would have fired. Instead, he dropped his gun and howled with pain. A knife, thrown at him by one of the passengers who had seized his chance to help, was sticking into his thigh.

A few hours later, the stage-coach rolled into the town of Del Rio. Soon all the townsfolk had heard the news of the captured robbers. A crowd gathered at the stagecoach office. Sheriff Wiatt had to push his way through.

"They wore gray hoods," the driver told him. The sheriff knew at once what that meant. They were part of the Cavendish gang.

The two robbers were led away, and John turned to go. Someone called his name. Turning, he saw Amy Striker, the pretty young woman whom he had made friends with on the stagecoach. Her uncle Lucas ran Del Rio's newspaper.

Lucas Striker wanted to shake John's hand for saving his niece from the outlaws, and Amy invited John to supper. There was more to Amy than just a pretty face, and he certainly wanted to know her better.

But John shook his head politely. "Thank you, I'd like to," he said, "but I can't tonight. I'm trying to reach the Ranger compound."

Lucas Striker raised his eyebrows. "Oh?" he asked. "Are you joining the Rangers?"

"No, sir," John answered with a smile. "I studied in the East to become a lawyer, not a lawman. I'm going to see my brother."

Dan Reid had changed a lot in the years since the two brothers had last seen each other. He wasn't just older. He was tired down to his very bones, almost beat.

There had been just too many years of fighting, as a soldier in the Confederate Army during the Civil War and as a Ranger chasing the Cavendish gang. There had been too many defeats. Cavendish had maybe one hundred riders to count on. Captain Dan Reid had only ten Rangers under his command. And Cavendish was smart. He had been a major in the Union Army during the Civil War. That was before he had been dishonorably discharged by General Grant for murder. Now he led the worst desperadoes — all killers — who had ever ridden the prairies and badlands of the Lone Star State of Texas.

Dan felt that he needed his brother. "Help us, John," he said. "Forget your lawbooks right now. You can't bring justice to Texas with them. Join the Rangers."

John slowly shook his head and hoped his brother would understand. "I was in the war too, Dan," he explained, "and I learned something. I don't ever want to kill another human being." It was the voice of the Great Mysterious speaking within him that caused him to talk that way.

Dan's face became grim. "Maybe you'll change your mind," he said, "if you know who's riding with Cavendish — some of the same rats who gunned down our ma and pa."

There was a long silence. Many feelings were welling up inside of John, and fighting to control them, he fell silent. When he finally answered, his voice was quiet, but it trembled with anger. "I still can't do it, Dan," he said.

Later that evening, the two brothers went into town with the Rangers. It was All Saints' Day, and everyone was having a wonderful time celebrating. There was Mexican music and dancing in the square. There was plenty of food, too, and make-believe skeletons filled with candy for the children to pop open with a stick.

There was something else to be excited about besides the fiesta. In a few weeks, Ulysses S. Grant—the President of the United States himself—was coming west for a buffalo hunt, and he was going to stop right there in Del Rio!

In the crowd, John met his friend Amy Striker. They smiled at each other. Dan could see that they wanted to be alone, so he excused himself and left them together.

"Do you dance?" Amy asked.

"Not very well," answered John shyly.

"Well, come on. I'll teach you," she said, and led John onto the dance floor.

While the young couple danced, the Rangers relaxed and joined

the party. After all, there was no reason to expect any trouble. No one had seen six men in gray hoods slipping quietly out of the shadows into the newspaper office where Lucas Striker and his assistant were working.

Moments later, a wounded man staggered into the crowd and fell to the ground. It was Lucas Striker's assistant. Dan and the Rangers rushed to the newspaper office. It had been wrecked. And Mr. Striker hung from a noose. Dan suspected at once who had murdered Amy's uncle. Striker had been writing articles in his newspaper against Cavendish.

"There's tracks, sir, six riders!" reported one of the Rangers.

"Mount up!" commanded Dan, and the Rangers sprang onto their horses.

Suddenly John swung up on a horse beside him. "I'm going with you," he said.

Dan looked at his brother and smiled. Now they were really together. "All right, men!" he shouted. "Let's get 'em!"

The men rode silently all night, following the tracks in the moonlight. By dawn they were in Indian territory. John said to his brother, "I'll help any way I can, but I won't shoot anyone." He hoped that the killers could be caught and brought to trial.

Dan shook his head. "Let me tell you about frontier justice, little brother," he said. "There is none. The judges are all crooks."

"I'll take my chances," John answered.

The horses stopped. The trail had led to the mouth of a narrow canyon called Bryant's Gap. High rocks rose on both sides of the entrance. Dan was worried about going inside. It was a perfect place for an ambush. Cavendish could be up there hidden behind the rocks with his men. Perhaps the real reason for Mr. Striker's murder was to trick the Rangers into coming there.

One of the Rangers, a man named Collins, stepped forward. "Maybe I should go in there and scout it out," he offered.

"Okay, Collins," said Dan, "but watch yourself."

"Always do, Captain," said Collins as he led his horse toward the canyon. "Yes, I always do," he said to himself.

While the other men waited in silence, Ranger Collins led his horse slowly up a steep, rocky cliff. Finally he reached the top and looked around.

Down below, Dan watched through his binoculars. Collins signaled to him that all was clear. Dan ordered his men to mount up. He flipped John a Ranger's badge. If there was going to be trouble, John ought to be a lawman. The badge made it legal. John pinned it on his chest. Whatever might happen, he was a Texas Ranger now! Dan led his men toward the canyon. Single file they rode through a shallow stream into the gap.

High above them, hiding with rifles cocked, were Butch Cavendish and thirty of his best sharpshooters. With them, ready to fire on the men below, was Ranger Collins—and Wiatt, the crooked

sheriff of Del Rio.

"Aim well, boys," Cavendish thought to himself. "These Rangers are all that stands between me and Ulysses S. Grant!"

As soon as his Rangers were in the canyon, Dan began to sense that something was wrong. Collins had not returned. Why? There was something in the air. . . .

"Let's get out of here!" Dan suddenly ordered.

The men started to turn back. But it was too late. From high above, huge boulders came rolling down to block the canyon's entrance. "Commence fire!" yelled Cavendish. The fight was on!

The Rangers were caught tight in a trap. They couldn't get out the way they had come in. They couldn't see the men firing at them. One by one, the sharpshooters picked the Rangers off.

Only the blinding dust kicked up by their frightened horses saved them from being finished off all at one time.

Dan realized that there was only one chance for them. They would have to race through the gunfire to the other side of the canyon. "This way!" he screamed, and spurred his horse. Only two Rangers were able to follow him. John tried too, but his horse was shot out from under him. He rushed for the cover of a rock.

Cavendish's men turned their guns on the fleeing Rangers. The bullets from thirty rifles fell around them as they raced across the floor of the canyon. Only one Ranger made it to the other side. It was Dan.

The Ranger Captain looked grim. Was he really the only one left? Then he heard gunfire still going on in the canyon. Someone was alive in there. Maybe it was John! He could not leave *any* of his men to fight it out alone. Turning, he galloped back into the canyon!

First a bullet struck him in the arm. Then his horse was hit, and Dan went flying. Suddenly a Ranger broke from the cover of a rock and came racing toward him. It was his brother.

"No, John! Stay down!" Dan screamed. But it was too late. John fell, wounded in the thigh. A moment later, John pulled himself to his feet and started to limp toward his brother. Another bullet —and he fell again.

Seeing John lying still on the ground, Dan broke from the cover of his dead horse. He made his way to his fallen brother. The two wounded brothers looked at each other with love in their eyes. They were saying good-bye. Another shot rang out and Dan slumped over. He was dead.

Standing on top of the ridge, Cavendish ordered Collins to go down and check things out. The man who had betrayed his fellow Rangers rode down to see if any Rangers were still breathing. But the traitor was so ashamed of what he had done that he didn't look very carefully. He did not see John's eyes open for an instant to stare at him, then close again as he fell unconscious.

For hours the canyon was still except for the hawks circling above it. At last, something else moved. An Indian hunter high up on the ridge was descending slowly into the gap.

As he passed among the fallen Rangers, a little gasping sound caught his ear. Someone was alive! Quickly, he got off his horse and went to the man. The Ranger was unconscious and barely breathing. The Indian knelt beside him to feel his pulse. Then he noticed something glitter on the man's chest. It was the silver amulet, the gift of long ago. Tonto had found his Kemo Sabe!

Since John was too weak to make the long journey back to the Indian village, Tonto carried him to a nearby cave that he often used while hunting. Laying John down gently on a blanket, Tonto built a small fire and left. Quickly he searched the hillside for the roots and herbs he needed to heal his friend.

Returning, he placed them in a kettle of boiling water in which he was cleaning his hunting knife.

Then Tonto took the knife and cut the bullets out of John's injured arm and leg. He was thankful that his friend was still unconscious and could not feel the pain.

Then he laid the steaming herbs and roots carefully over John's wounds. They were the remedies that his people had been using for ages. Many a brave, wounded by an arrow or a buffalo —or later, the bullet of a paleface soldier—had been saved by them.

But medicine was not enough. Deep into the night, Tonto danced around the body of his sleeping friend. As he danced, he chanted a prayer to the healing powers of the Great Mysterious.

Dawn came and passed. The sun rose high in the sky. But still the wounded man did not waken. Tonto's watchful eyes were growing heavy and he feared for his friend. Tonto was nodding when he heard a sound. It was John. A word was forming on his lips. Tonto leaned forward.

"Dan?" John murmured in his sleep.

Kneeling beside him, Tonto wiped the beads of sweat from John's face and waited for him to open his eyes.

"Dan!" John cried again, trying in his dream to save his brother. It was the sound of his own voice that woke him with a start. Bewildered, he looked around. He didn't know where he was or who had brought him here. Now the face of an Indian with gentle eyes was hovering close to him, reminding him to be still and to rest.

"Kemo Sabe," said Tonto.

"Tonto?" John asked at last.

"Yes," came the answer, "Tonto."

Slowly, John closed his eyes again and fell into a peaceful sleep. He was safe.

It was several days before John was strong enough to be moved to Tonto's village. Tonto tied John to a kind of stretcher which dragged behind his horse.

When they finally arrived, John was surprised at what he saw. Gone were most of the tepees. Gone, too, were the happy faces, the playing children, the squaws working on hides, and old Chief Talking Bear. The village looked half destroyed.

"Tonto, what happened here?" he asked.

"Soldiers," Tonto answered, and said no more.

He didn't have to. John understood that the promises of the paleface chiefs had been broken many times. Again and again the soldiers had taken from the Indians what had been theirs. And when the Indians had fought back, their villages were destroyed. This was what was left of Tonto's home.

That night in the council lodge, Tonto spoke of these things. Many of the braves did not want John Reid to stay among them. "I know what has been done to us," said Tonto, "but the man who I have brought here is a brother—and I will defend his life with my own if need be." Then Tonto remembered the wisdom of Chief Talking Bear and he said, "Let him be judged not by his color but by his heart." The council stirred. They agreed that Tonto had spoken that which was just. Once more, Tonto's Kemo Sabe would be welcome among them.

While John was recovering, he spent a lot of time thinking about what had happened to the Rangers. Now he was the only one left—the lone Ranger—except for Collins, the traitor. John had lost his father and mother, and now his brother, to outlaws. He hated Cavendish with all his heart. He decided he had to hunt him down.

This decision worried Tonto. Had John not vowed that he would kill no human being? And was it not the white man's law that a criminal should have a trial?

John would not listen to his friend. "He must die," he said. That was all there was to it.

While John's right arm was still in a sling, he began preparing for his next encounter with Cavendish. He would need to be able to shoot accurately with both hands to face the Cavendish gang. But learning to shoot with his left hand was hard. His practice shots always just missed the bull's-eye.

"Here," said Tonto as John was about to reload his six-shooter, "try these." In the brave's outstretched hand were bullets different from any John had ever seen. They were made of pure silver.

John took one, loaded his gun, aimed, and fired. Bull's-eye! He was delighted and surprised. Tonto explained that the chiefs of old had tipped their arrows with silver to make them fly straighter.

"They will help your aim be true," he said. "But use them wisely, Kemo Sabe, for among us, silver stands for that which is just."

A few days later, John threw away his sling. His wounded arm was almost healed. All it needed now was exercise. Swimming would help. John began swimming every day in the lake near the village.

One day as he was swimming toward the shore, he saw a shimmering reflection in the water. He stopped swimming and looked up.

Standing on the shore was a white stallion. It was the most beautiful horse John had ever seen. The horse stood still as a statue, watching John.

"Well, good morning!" said John pleasantly.

At the sound of John's voice, the stallion pranced a few steps, then turned and raced away.

Early the next morning John and Tonto were just stepping into a clearing when they saw the white horse. In the misty light, the horse seemed to glow.

"Look at him," said John.

"He shines like the moon," said Tonto.

"Like silver," said John.

Unaware that he was being watched, the magnificent stallion ran free as the wind in the clearing. Silently, Tonto and John crept nearer the horse. John's heart began to pound. He wanted that horse. But could he catch and tame the wild beast?

The horse allowed John to approach him slowly. But at the first touch of John's hand, he bolted.

"Silver!" John called, for that was the name he decided to give the stallion. Almost as if the horse accepted his new name, he stopped and waited to see what would happen next. "Steady. Steady, big fellow," John said softly as he moved in closer to stroke the animal's neck. Tonto followed behind. In his hands were a blanket, a coil of rope, and a saddle. Carefully, John reached back and took the blanket from Tonto. Then he tossed it over the stallion's head.

Now that the horse was unable to see what was going on, Tonto threw the saddle over his back and slid the rope over his head. John swung quickly up onto the saddle, and the blanket was yanked away.

For a second the huge horse stood still. Then, in a snort of fury, he pawed the air, hit the ground, bucked, and burst into a run. Horse and rider streaked out of the clearing. Over boulders, around trees, down steep trails they went. Silver tried every way he could to throw John off. Then the stallion stopped short. John went flying, but not completely off. He managed to hang onto the stallion's neck and hold on for dear life.

Silver would not give up. Faster and faster he ran. John didn't realize until too late that they were heading straight for a cliff! He tried to rein in the horse, but nothing could stop Silver now. Off the cliff they went, then down, down, down to the rushing river below.

Rising to the surface, John fought against the racing current and made it to the shallow water. He dragged himself out of the river and fell down to rest.

When he finally looked up, there was Silver. The white stallion was waiting for him! John had not conquered the horse. He had not wanted to. But they were friends now. John climbed back on Silver and rode him into the Indian village.

Several weeks had passed after the ambush at Bryant's Gap. The time came for John to make his move against Cavendish. The outlaw leader must have had some reason for wanting Dan and his men out of the way. Some big plan must be afoot. Whatever it was, John suspected it would be put into action soon. How could he find out?

It might be best, John thought, not to let Cavendish know that any of the Rangers had escaped alive. If he showed up in Del Rio, someone would be sure to recognize him. . . . Suddenly, John reached a decision. John Reid would no longer exist. In his place would be a man whom no one knew—a man in a mask.

That night, the two friends visited the place where Tonto had buried Dan and the other Rangers. It was time for Cavendish and his murderous gang to pay in full. For the first time in his life, John Reid put on the mask that forever turned a young lawyer and lawman into the Lone Ranger.

Later that night, the Lone Ranger and Tonto rode into Del Rio. The masked man was ready to start getting some big questions answered. Sheriff Wiatt and his deputy were sitting in their office at the Del Rio jail. The sheriff was hopping mad at Amy Striker. She had written another attack on him for not going after the Cavendish gang. "If she's gonna continue where her uncle left off," said Wiatt, "she's gonna end up where he did—dead." Neither the sheriff nor the deputy noticed that a masked man had entered quietly and may have overheard.

"Sheriff Wiatt?" said the Lone Ranger.

Wiatt and the deputy were startled. The sheriff reached for his gun. "The mask—take it off!" he ordered.

"That won't be necessary," said the Lone Ranger as Tonto appeared out of nowhere to back him up. The sheriff and his deputy got the point—and the deputy eased away from his gun.

"Can you tell me when Cavendish was last seen?" the Lone Ranger asked. "Have there been any more raids?"

The sheriff looked closely at the stranger. He was trying to figure him out. "You ask a lot of questions for a masked man," he answered. "No. Nobody's seen Cavendish."

The Lone Ranger's next question really made the sheriff nervous. "What about Eddie Collins, the Texas Ranger?"

"Why? What's he got to do with it?" asked the sheriff suspiciously.

"Nothing," the Lone Ranger pretended. "We were soldiers together a long time ago."

"Probably find him in the cantina," the deputy said. The sheriff threw a nasty look at the deputy, but it was too late now.

"Thanks," said the Lone Ranger, and he left with Tonto.

Sure enough, Eddie Collins was in the cantina. As usual, he was getting drunk as quickly as possible. It didn't bother him too much to see a man in a mask come in and sit down at his table. He playfully put up his hands and pretended that it was a holdup. Soon, though, he stopped thinking that it was so funny. The masked man was staring hard at him and saying, "I want you to take me to Cavendish."

Collins nearly fell out of his seat. "How would I know Cavendish?" he half whispered.

"Because you led those Rangers to him. Now lead me."

Collins paled with fear. "You're crazy!" he cried. "I don't know Cavendish! I don't know what you're talking about!"

With a shaking hand, he poured himself another drink. But a barrel of whiskey couldn't help the traitor now. There was no escaping the look in the eyes of the masked man. Collins could sense that somehow this man knew all about the part he had played in the ambush of Dan and his men.

Now the Lone Ranger demanded to know what the real reason for the ambush was. What plan did Cavendish have that first required wiping out all of the Texas Rangers in the area?

From the shadows outside the cantina, Sheriff Wiatt stood and watched. He had followed the Lone Ranger from the jail. Now his worst fears seemed about to come true. Collins was becoming more and more terrified of the masked man. In another minute, he would spill everything. Carefully, the sheriff raised his pistol and took aim.

Meanwhile, the Lone Ranger was putting on the pressure. "Tell me the truth, Collins," he said. "It's your only salvation."

Collins could hold back no longer. "Cavendish?" he blurted out, "he wants the train . . . he wants . . ." A shot rang out and Collins fell forward, never to finish his sentence.

The sheriff smiled to himself. He could pin Collins's murder on the masked man and his Indian friend. Shoving his gun into Tonto's back, Wiatt pushed him into the cantina. Using Tonto as a shield, Wiatt intended to arrest the masked man as well. But he was too late. The Lone Ranger had vanished.

The word spread like wildfire through the town. Ranger Collins had been shot in the back by an Indian. What did the town need a trial for? He was a redskin, wasn't he? He *must* be guilty. "I say we string him up! Hang him!" shouted the sheriff's stooge. The mob rushed toward the jail.

The deputy stared out the jailhouse window, then called back to Tonto in his cell, "Hey, Crazy Horse! You're going to the happy hunting grounds."

Grinning to himself, Wiatt went outside the jailhouse and pretended to calm the crowd. "Just hold it right there," he said.

The sheriff's friend pointed a gun at him, shouting, "Don't get in the way, Wiatt! We're taking the Indian. Step aside!"

Wiatt did just that, and the leaders of the mob rushed inside. When they came out again, it was with Tonto. His hands were tied behind his back as he walked, mutely enduring the curses and blows of the howling mob. He was determined to die in silence. They would not see him cringe. Tonto was at peace with the Great Mysterious. His silence infuriated the mob even more.

Two men shoved him up the wooden steps that led to the gallows. They placed the noose around his neck. Below him was a trap door. Once they opened it, he would fall through—and the noose would kill him.

Now, one of the sheriff's stooges reached for the handle that would open that trap door. Suddenly, the handle no longer existed! A silver bullet had blown it to pieces.

"Come on, Silver!" shouted the Lone Ranger as he came riding like the wind, his two guns blazing. The sheriff's six-shooter was shot out of his hand before he could aim it. The mob was too slow for the great stallion and the man who rode him. Another silver bullet cut the rope above Tonto's head. The white horse streaked past the gallows and Tonto leaped onto it behind his Kemo Sabe. The cry "Hi-yo, Silver!" filled the air. Horse, Indian, and masked man were gone.

At camp that night, far from Del Rio and safe from the sheriff, the Lone Ranger thought over the words of Ranger Collins. "He wants the train. . . ." Yes, but what train does Cavendish want? And why?

The next morning the Lone Ranger and Tonto mounted their horses and set off for Del Rio. Somehow they had to discover what Cavendish's plan was—before it was too late.

Amy Striker was hurrying down the street toward the town hall when a little Mexican boy came running up to her.

"Senorita, there's a padre who wants to see you in the church right away," he said. "He says it's important."

Amy went to the old Spanish church. Inside it was so dark that she could see nothing for a minute. Then she saw a monk stand-ing in the shadows near the confessional box. He beckoned to her.

"Your newspaper writings," he began, "they're very brave, but also dangerous. I am here to tell you that there is someone who wants to help you in your fight against Cavendish."

There was something familiar about this monk's voice. Amy moved closer to try to see the face shrouded in the hooded robe. Just then another monk entered the church.

"Please, in here," said the monk whose voice sounded familiar. He motioned Amy into the confessional box. Inside the confessional, Amy and the monk were just inches apart. The black confessional curtain hung between them.

"In my travels, I met a man who wears a mask, but is dedicated to law and order," said the monk through the curtain. "He wants you to know that he will not stop until he has brought Cavendish to justice."

"Well, until he gets Cavendish, I'll just continue my writing," said Amy.

"No, you mustn't," said the monk firmly. "You'll get hurt."

"Cavendish has already hurt me," said Amy. "I lost my uncle and somebody else whom I care for deeply. Now, Father, you must excuse me. I'm late for the town meeting. We are planning for President Grant's arrival."

"The president of the United States! He's coming here?" asked the monk in a stunned voice.

"Why yes, on the afternoon train today. And he's bringing General Custer and Wild Bill Hickok and Buffalo Bill. It's quite an event for this little town."

"So that's what he's after," mumbled the monk.

"What did you say?" asked Amy.

"I must go now. Trust the masked rider, Amy," said the monk.

Amy could hear the monk leaving the confessional box and running quickly down the aisle to the door. "Wait!" she called, but he was gone. She had not seen this strange monk's face, but she felt sure she knew him. Then she brushed the confessional curtain aside and saw a shiny object lying on the floor. It was a silver bullet.

A few minutes later, a man wearing a mask and an Indian interrupted the town meeting.

"Cavendish is going after the President's train," the Lone Ranger warned. "We need men to ride with us and stop him."

"Why should we listen to the likes of you?" cried the mayor. Then voices began to buzz. Ranger Collins was killed by a redskin who was helped by a masked man!

The Lone Ranger tried to reason with them, but there was no time for explanations. "If we had killed Collins," he said, "we wouldn't have come back." People shook their heads. How could they believe a masked man?

Amy Striker, who was covering the meeting for her newspaper, stepped forward. "I don't understand you people!" she shouted. "Can't you hear what this man is saying? There's going to be an attack on the President's life! And we are the only ones who can do anything about it!"

The Lone Ranger was proud of Amy. He wished he could tell her who he really was. Perhaps she had already guessed.

One by one, everyone there who could help out made a different excuse. "I . . . uh . . . I got a wife and kids," said one fellow. "That's what we got a sheriff for," said another. It was no use.

The Lone Ranger and Tonto spurred their horses. They alone had to save President Ulysses S. Grant. Following the railroad tracks, they headed east.

The President of the United States was sitting in his private car—the last car on the train—writing a speech. He looked up when Buffalo Bill Cody, Wild Bill Hickok, and General Custer entered. They were all looking forward to the buffalo hunt.

"As long as we're going hunting," said General Custer, "maybe we can get some Indians and buffalo at the same time while we're out here."

Everyone thought it was a good joke. Even the President really believed that the Indians were the cause of most of the trouble in the West. He didn't know that there were only two people in Del Rio

long hose that hung from it was slowly dipping down as the train came closer.

When the engine rolled past the tower, Cavendish's men slid down the hose onto the roof of the train. Seconds later, the man in the tree landed on the roof too. The plan was in operation, but the Lone Ranger and Tonto were nowhere in sight!

The President, meanwhile, was in the dining car eating his lunch. Finishing, he rose and walked back to his private car. As the train climbed uphill toward a tunnel, the outlaws quietly climbed down into the open space between the two cars. Working swiftly, they pulled out the big metal spike that kept the President's car connected to the rest of the train.

By the time the train entered the tunnel, it was like a worm that had been cut in two. All the cars but one were winding westward toward Del Rio. The President's car was rushing back eastward to where the outlaw chief waited with his gang.

It was hours before the Lone Ranger arrived at the scene of the President's capture. The car was deserted. Everyone was gone.

Tonto examined the ground. "There are many horses, many men," he said grimly.

"Let's go!" said the Lone Ranger. They swung onto their horses and galloped off after the desperadoes.

willing to risk their lives to save his —and one of them was an Indian.

While the President's train rolled westward, Butch Cavendish and his gang rode up to the tracks farther ahead. He ordered three of his men to climb into a water tower next to the tracks. Another man climbed onto a limb of a tree hanging over the tracks. Cavendish and the rest of his men stayed out of sight.

Soon the train appeared in the distance. The engineer was too busy running the train to pay attention to an old water tower up ahead. He didn't notice that the

It was well into the night before the Lone Ranger and Tonto found Cavendish's fortlike hide-out. A wall of twenty-foot-high logs, sharpened at the top like spears, surrounded it. Not far away was a high guardpost. To get inside, they would have to find a way to fool the sentry. But how?

Tonto had an idea. Silently he climbed a cliff behind the guard until he was looking down at the several buildings of the outlaw's camp. He carefully sent a few rocks tumbling noisily into the camp.

"What's that about?" the guard wondered, looking around. While Tonto kept the guard distracted with falling rocks, the Lone Ranger went into action. Taking a rope from his saddle, he tied a small rock to one end. He tossed the rope, hooking it around the top of one of the logs. With Silver's help, the masked man climbed the fence and slowly lowered himself to the ground on the other side. Then he hid in the trees near a stream running through the compound and waited for Tonto to join him.

In one of the buildings the outlaw chief had been entertaining his prisoner with a meal fit for a President. After the table was cleared, brandy was served and cigars were passed around. Then Cavendish read aloud a letter he was going to send to the government.

The letter said that if America wanted its President back alive, it would have to give up the state of Texas. That meant people, land, cattle—everything. He, Butch Cavendish, would become the sole ruler of a new empire in the West. The United States had just thirty days to make up its mind to turn over Texas—or else.

"Sign as witness," ordered Cavendish, shoving the letter and a pen at Grant.

President Grant had been a tough and a brave soldier most of his life. He was not afraid of the madman in front of him. But he knew better than to oppose him just then. So he took the pen and signed the letter.

Meanwhile, the Lone Ranger and Tonto made their way up the stream into the center of the outlaws' camp. A bunkhouse lay in front of them now. Men were going in and out of it. The outlaws could spot them at any moment. Where could they hide?

A shed! The two friends raced through the shadows to the door of the little building. But it was locked! Noises were coming from the bunkhouse. The glow of a cigarette appeared in the bunkhouse door. They were about to be seen!

Tonto suddenly realized that the hinges on the shed door were made of leather, not metal. Two swift slashes with his hunting knife and the door opened. Plunging inside, they looked around them. It was the ammunition shed. What luck! Until now, the Lone Ranger had no clear idea how to rescue the President. But here was the answer—dynamite!

Waiting until all the lights were out in the camp, the Lone Ranger and Tonto slipped out of the shed with bundles of explosives. Quickly they darted from building to building in the camp and placed their sticks of dynamite. Those were for later. First they had to find the President.

The President, thought the Lone Ranger, must be in the main house with Cavendish himself. Moving around the side of the building, the two friends tried the windows. Locked. Suddenly they froze. Hoofbeats. Two of Cavendish's men were riding their way. On a hunch, the Lone Ranger tried the side door. It opened!

Once inside, they moved swiftly and silently around the main floor. No one was there. They climbed the stairs. The main hallway was deserted. Every door was closed. In which room was the President being kept prisoner? There was no way to tell. They turned a corner—and ran right into a guard.

The Lone Ranger's fist knocked the guard unconscious. The masked man and Tonto opened the nearest door and dragged him inside to hide him. They found themselves in a bedroom—with Sheriff Wiatt himself peacefully sleeping on the bed.

The Lone Ranger shook Wiatt roughly. "Time for you to get up, Sheriff."

Wiatt opened his eyes and stared at the masked man.

"Where's the President?" the Lone Ranger asked.

"I don't know," Wiatt lied.

Tonto stepped forward and unsheathed his knife.

"Third door down on the left! He's in there!" cried Wiatt.

With Wiatt and the guard safely tied and gagged, they entered Grant's room. The President was asleep and the Lone Ranger woke him gently.

"We're here to help," said the Lone Ranger.

The President looked up at the masked man. "You don't look like the kind that's going to help me," he said. "And neither does he."

"Trust us," said the Lone Ranger, handing him Sheriff Wiatt's gunbelt. "Put on your clothes, Mr. President. We're taking you home."

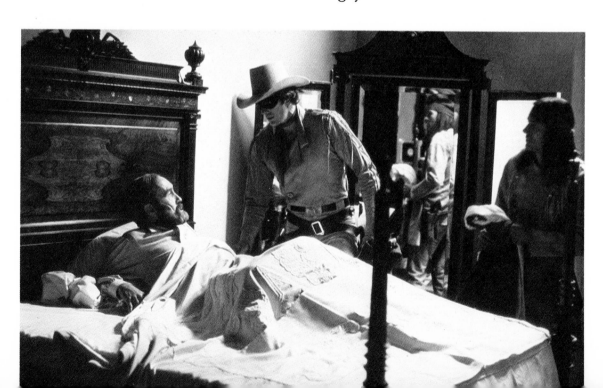

The President of the United States hurried to get dressed. They would have to move quickly. It was already becoming daylight. Soon the whole camp would be awake. But the Lone Ranger had prepared for that.

Rushing out of the main building, Tonto and the Lone Ranger began lighting the fuses that would set off the explosives. When the President saw what they were doing, he eagerly joined in. They were almost finished when a siren blasted the air. They were discovered! The three men raced for the corral where the outlaws kept their horses.

When the alarm went off, the men inside the bunkhouse tumbled out of their cots. Reaching for their gun belts, they stumbled toward the door. A sudden blast —and both door and stairway vanished in front of them. The men fell back inside.

Taking advantage of the dust and confusion, the three companions leaped onto horses belonging to the outlaws and galloped headlong toward the main gates. Suddenly a shot rang out and the President's horse fell, sending Grant sprawling into the stream.

The shot came from Cavendish's rifle. He was standing at the main house getting ready to fire again. Quickly the Lone Ranger wheeled about and dashed to the President's side. Lifting him up, the Lone Ranger turned his horse and, with Grant hanging on behind him, headed for the main gates.

Within a few seconds the rest of the dynamite began exploding. First at the back of the main building. Then at the barn. Then at the corral, scattering the horses. Cavendish's plans were going up in smoke, but he still had his rifle. He could still kill. He leveled his rifle at the horse carrying the Lone Ranger and Grant. Crack! The horse fell and its two riders went sprawling headlong into the stream. Now they were helpless. Cavendish leveled his rifle again. It looked as if nothing could stop him from killing the President of the United States and the Lone Ranger now. But a cloud of dense black smoke suddenly poured out of the burning building, surrounding him.

At last, the Lone Ranger saw his chance to get the man who had murdered his brother and the

Rangers. He helped the President to a safe hiding place. Then he raced back toward the outlaw camp. Breaking free of the smoke, Cavendish saw him coming—and fired.

Meanwhile, Tonto had set a little wooden box afloat on the stream. In it were several sticks of dynamite with a long, slow-burning fuse. The whole escape plan depended on that one little fuse. The dynamite was headed for the main gates. But the fuse sputtered and went out. Cavendish's men were out of the bunkhouse now. They fired at Tonto as he raced down to the box with a burning ember in his hand. But he made it! And as he relighted the fuse, he had no time to pay attention to a sound in the distance.

President Grant heard it clearly. It was the bugle cry of his own United States Cavalry! Grant smiled. He had expected the cavalry to be called into action the moment it was discovered that the presidential car was missing. But if the mysterious masked man and his Indian friend had not stepped in first, the cavalry would have been too late to prevent Cavendish's plan from working.

At the head of the troops, Custer, Cody, and Hickok led the charge. All that stood between them now and the already confused outlaws were the towering main gates. Suddenly there was a tremendous explosion. The main gates blew into a million pieces and the cavalry poured through.

It was all over, and Cavendish knew it. Breaking off his gun battle with the Lone Ranger, he jumped on a horse and galloped away. The Lone Ranger whistled. Instantly, Silver was there. He had come through the gates with the cavalry to find his master. Now the two took off after Cavendish.

Cavendish's horse was no match for the great white stallion. Overtaking Cavendish, the Lone Ranger leaped from his saddle— dragging Cavendish with him to the ground. They fought like tigers. At last the masked man pinned Cavendish to the ground.

And now the last of the Rangers drew his gun. Here was the man who had murdered his brother, the man he had sworn to kill. He raised the pistol to the outlaw's head.

"What are you waiting for?" gasped Cavendish. "Do it!"

Perhaps the Lone Ranger was thinking of an earlier promise he had made to himself. Or perhaps he heard the voice of the Great Mysterious. He could not kill this man in cold blood. He would leave him to the law.

The President of the United States was very grateful to the Lone Ranger and Tonto. He wanted to know the real name of the masked man. He wanted the whole world to know the name of the man who had saved him.

The Lone Ranger shook his head. It would be better if he remained unknown, in order to continue his work.

The President turned to Tonto. How could he best thank him?

Tonto remembered his village and what soldiers had done to it. "Thank me, great chief," he said, "by honoring your treaties with my people."

The President was silent for a moment, then answered, "Yes, we will try."

Saying good-bye, the Lone Ranger shook the President's hand. As he did so, he pressed something into Grant's palm. After watching the two friends ride away, the President looked at what had been placed in his hand. It was a silver bullet.

"Who in thunderation *is* that masked man?" he asked.

"Why that's—" said General Custer, "that's—I really don't know, sir."

From off in the distance came the cry that would be heard again and again across the West:

"HI-YO, SILVER. AWAY!"